This book is to be returned on or before
the last date stamped b

URAL

CKED

LIBREX

First published in Great Britain by
A & C. Black (Publishers) Ltd 1990
First published in Young Lions 1991
Reprinted twice in 1992

Young Lions is an imprint of the Children's Division,
part of HarperCollins Publishers Ltd,
77–85 Fulham Palace Road, Hammersmith, London W6 8JB

Copyright © Colin West 1990

Printed and bound in Great Britain by
HarperCollins Manufacturing, Glasgow

Monty Gets the Chop

Simon and Josie Sprod were worried that Monty was just as clumsy as ever.

It was only an old vase, anyway.

They'd made Monty a pair of glasses to remind him to look where he was going, but he still seemed accident-prone.

'From now on, every time you cause an accident, we're going to put it in the book,' said Simon.

'And if you get three mishaps in one day, you're in for the chop!' said Josie.

Monty had to make sure he was
extra careful from now on.
He walked round the house
very cautiously.

But then at lunchtime, Monty was careless. When getting a sausage that someone had left on their plate . . .

. . . he pulled off the tablecloth . . .

. . . and most of the things on it.

It all went down in the book.

Later, on his way to the garden,
Monty knocked over the pot plant
in the hall.

That went down in the book, too.

Monty was really worried now.
One more mishap, and he'd be in for
the chop.

He hardly dared move, in case he
knocked something over, or spilled
something, or put his foot in
something.

In the end, Monty just sat in his basket while Mrs Sprod got on with the cooking.

You're very quiet this evening, Monty. Are you all right?

Before Monty could open his mouth, Mrs Sprod took a dish from the oven. It smelled delicious.

9

'Oh dear, I've cooked too much
meat,' murmured Mrs Sprod.
'Here, Monty, as you're being so good,
you can have the chop.'

'How very confusing!' thought
Monty as he licked his lips.

Monty's Picnic

It was a beautiful sunny day and the Sprod family were going on a picnic. Monty was dozing in his basket.

'Now, have I got everything?' asked Mrs Sprod as she examined the hamper.

Vacuum flask, plastic cups, serviettes, egg sandwiches, mince pies...

Suddenly Monty sat up.

Did someone say **mince pies**?

Mr Sprod took the hamper to the car.
Simon and Josie helped to tie it on.

Mrs Sprod locked up the house and
then they were off.

The Sprods' house

They went for miles and miles and miles and miles.

To the Seaside

N
W E
S

14

And after two hours . . .

Mrs Sprod noticed they were getting low on petrol.

Josie spotted a garage.

Mrs Sprod drew up and got out to work the pump. Mr Sprod and the children went to investigate the shop.

When Mrs Sprod went to pay
at the till, Monty clambered through
a back window . . .

. . . and on to the roof of the car.

He sniffed the hamper.

There was no stopping him.
He nudged open the lid, hopped in
and got to work on the pies.

By the time Monty was on his fifth mince pie, he heard voices from below.

Crikey! They're back already.

Before he could do anything, the car started up.

VRROOOOM!

Monty held on to the sides of the
hamper as the car sped along.
He only just managed to duck in
time for a bridge.

They went round lots of bends...

...and lots of over bumps.

MEANWHILE, back inside the car...

'Is Monty enjoying the ride?' asked
Mrs Sprod. For the first time,
Simon and Josie looked down at
the empty space between them.

'WHAT!' exclaimed Mr Sprod.
The car screeched to a halt.

It was such a sudden jolt that
Monty and the picnic food were
hurled from the hamper.

Mr Sprod got out. He was quite angry.

That dog must have been sitting inside the hamper.

Monty looked ill.

'Let's go to the sea-side anyway,'
said Mrs Sprod. 'We'll find a nice
snack bar.'

So that's what they did.

But guess who couldn't eat another thing all day!

Monty and the Cat Next Door

Gertrude, the cat next door, was really getting on Monty's nerves. She got all the attention these days.

One afternoon, Gertrude was preening herself by her front gate. Monty had noticed her through a gap in the fence.

Monty squeezed through the gap
and crept up behind Gertrude.

Then he let out his most ferocious
bark.

RRRUUFFF!

The terrified cat almost jumped out
of her skin.

Monty yapped some more, and the cat took off. Gertrude leapt through the bars of the front gate.

Monty set off after her.

But he wasn't quite as slim as
Gertrude. His head got through the
bars, but not the rest of him.

Try as he might, he couldn't budge.

Before long, a small crowd gathered round Monty.

Then a woman with a shopping
basket had a bright idea.

Carefully, she removed Monty's
glasses. Then she rubbed some
margarine behind his ears.

Monty simply pulled his head free!

Everyone cheered and made a
tremendous fuss of him.

And Monty was the talk of the
neighbourhood for weeks.

Monty and the School Fête

It was the day of Josie and Simon's school fête. All the proceeds were going to the School Orchestra Fund. Lots of stalls had been set up on the school playing field.

There were unusual games with
prizes for the lucky winners . . .

There was a white elephant stall.

There was a home-made cake stall.

There was a second-hand book stall.

And there was Simon and Josie's craft stall.

They'd made little animals out of
scraps of material . . .

ONLY 50p. EACH

. . . and paper-weights out of pebbles.

Hand painted

They'd knitted egg cosies . . .

IDEAL GIFT!

. . . and they'd made interesting jewellery out of bits and pieces.

The trouble was, not many people seemed interested in buying anything from them.

At half past three, the headmistress, Mrs Prendlethorpe, came along to see how things were going. Mrs P had met Monty before.

'Hello, Miss,' said Simon and Josie.
'Hello, children!' Mrs Prendlethorpe
said, trying to ignore Monty.

Then she looked down. 'Just keep
your dog out of mischief,' she said to
Simon in a quiet voice.

Monty heard Mrs Prendlethorpe
say she was off to help out at the
cake stall. He decided to follow her.

If I can get
into her good books,
I might get some
free samples!

But then, as Monty was wondering
how he could impress the
headmistress, a sudden gust of wind
almost knocked him off his feet.

Whoash!

The gust swept off Mrs P's hat, and carried it away.

Help! My new hat!

Monty seized his chance and chased
after the hat.

He raced through the crowds.

He had to run fast, but was just about
able to keep up with it.

Then, with one almighty leap,
Monty pounced and caught the hat
in his teeth!

A loud cheer went up. When Monty looked round, he saw that everyone had been watching him.

Monty made his way back to the cake stall, and returned the hat to Mrs Prendlethorpe. She seemed to be the only person who wasn't smiling.

Simon came over and apologised.
He took Monty back to the craft stall.

Josie sat Monty on a chair, so she could keep an eye on him. But she soon noticed people coming over to meet the dog who'd saved the headmistress's hat.

And everyone who came wanted to buy a souvenir.

By the end of the afternoon, Simon and Josie had sold everything in sight! They were able to hand over £37·97 for the School Orchestra Fund. The good news cheered up Mrs Prendlethorpe no end.

Monty's Mistake

One Friday afternoon, Mrs Sprod was reading a magazine . . .

. . . Josie was reading a book . . .

. . . and Simon was reading a comic.

Mrs Sprod was reading about diets.
Suddenly she said:

I'm very worried about your father. According to this article, he's nearly two stones overweight.

Just then Monty passed by the door.

Mrs Sprod went on:

Monty thought Mrs Sprod was
talking about *him!*

'I think you
should cut
down on his
sausages, too!'
said Josie.
'Good idea,'
said Mrs Sprod.

'And don't give
him so much
fruit cake!'
said Simon.
'That's a good
idea, too,'
said Mrs Sprod.

Monty gulped some more.
He didn't like the sound of this.

Monty plodded off and wondered
what to do.

But then he'd miss his comfy basket.

At last, Monty decided he'd have to
show everyone that although he
was podgy, he was still super-fit.

Monty prepared himself for his first
move. That evening, when Mr Sprod
came home from work, Monty
bounded down the garden path
and almost knocked him over.

Then Monty started yapping loudly.

Then he started dancing round
Mr Sprod, and even managed a few
somersaults.

He's never done that before.

Then he raced round Simon
seven times.

Monty was getting tired, but he
decided to do his most spectacular
feat of all . . .

He jumped up on to the bird bath
and tried to do a hand stand . . .

Unfortunately, Monty lost his balance and toppled into the pond.

Simon pulled out a bedraggled Monty.

Everyone crowded round Monty,
who was shivering.

So Josie took Monty inside.

Josie tucked Monty up, snug and warm. Then she fetched the biscuits.

Monty was amazed. His plan had worked after all!